Morgana Thorne

Bloodlines of Eternity

Bloodlines of Eternity

by

Morgana Thorne

Morgana Thorne

To my mother,

A true lover of vampire novels and the one who inspired my passion for storytelling. Your boundless imagination and unwavering support have been the guiding light on this journey. This book is for you, with all my love and gratitude.

Bloodlines of Eternity

Table of Contents

Prologue

In the dimly lit chamber of an ancient castle, flickering torchlight cast eerie shadows on the stone walls. A group of hooded figures gathered around a massive wooden table; their faces obscured by darkness. At the center of the table lay an old, leather-bound book, its pages yellowed with age. The leader of the group, a tall figure with piercing blue eyes, stepped forward and opened the book to a specific page.

"The prophecy speaks of a Bloodline of Eternity," the leader intoned, his voice echoing through the chamber. "A lineage that will either save or doom us all."

The others murmured in agreement, their voices a mix of fear and anticipation.

"In every generation, a child of this bloodline will be born, possessing powers beyond imagination," the leader continued. "We must ensure that this child is protected, for their destiny is intertwined with our own."

The group nodded solemnly; their resolve unyielding. For centuries, they had worked in secret, guarding the delicate balance between humans and vampires. The Veil had been their shield, keeping the world from descending into chaos.

But now, as the stars aligned and the signs of the prophecy began to unfold, they knew their greatest challenge was yet to come.

Chapter 1
A Strange Beginning

Elara Green's alarm clock buzzed incessantly, jolting her awake from a restless sleep. She groaned, slapping the snooze button before rolling over to stare at the ceiling. Another day in the bustling city of New Orleans awaited her, filled with the mundane tasks of her job at the local bookstore. Yet, beneath the veneer of her ordinary life, Elara felt a constant undercurrent of strangeness, a feeling she couldn't quite shake.

She dragged herself out of bed, her movements sluggish and heavy. As she glanced at her reflection in the mirror, she noticed the familiar, unsettling glow in her eyes. It had always been there, a subtle luminescence that set her apart, though she had learned to hide it well enough.

After a quick shower and a hurried breakfast, Elara left her small apartment and headed to the bookstore. The morning air was crisp, carrying the scent of blooming magnolias and the distant hum of the city waking up. She found solace in the routine of her work, the quiet comfort of being surrounded by books and stories that offered an escape from her own reality.

Midway through her shift, as she was stacking a new shipment of novels, the bell above the door chimed. Elara looked up to see a tall, dark-haired man entering the store. There was something striking about him, a presence that commanded attention. He moved with a grace and confidence that was almost otherworldly.

"Can I help you?" Elara asked, her curiosity piqued.

The man approached the counter, his eyes locking onto hers with an intensity that made her heart skip a beat. "I'm looking for a book," he said, his voice smooth and deep.

"It's quite old, and rather rare. Perhaps you have it in your collection."

Elara nodded, feeling a strange pull toward this mysterious stranger. "What's the title?"

"It's called 'The Veil and the Bloodline,'" he replied, a faint smile playing on his lips.

Her breath caught in her throat. She had heard of that book, a tome of ancient lore rumored to hold secrets about a hidden world. "I think we might have a copy in the back," she said, trying to keep her voice steady. "Let me check."

As Elara turned to head to the storage room, she felt the man's gaze following her, an unsettling mix of curiosity and expectation. She rummaged through the dusty shelves, finally locating the worn, leather-bound volume. The moment she touched it, a strange sensation washed over her, like a jolt of electricity.

Returning to the counter, she handed the book to the man, who accepted it with a nod of gratitude. "Thank you, Elara," he said, his use of her name surprising her. "This book is more important than you know."

Before she could ask how he knew her name, the man turned and left, leaving her with a sense of foreboding and a hundred unanswered questions. As she watched him disappear into the bustling streets, Elara felt a shift in the air, as if the very fabric of her reality was beginning to unravel.

Little did she know, this encounter was the first step in uncovering a destiny that would change her life forever.

Chapter 2
Unveiling Secrets

Clara couldn't shake the encounter with the mysterious man from her mind. His piercing eyes, the way he knew her name, and the old book he took with him—it all felt like the beginning of something monumental. That evening, after closing up the bookstore, she took the long way home, hoping the cool night air would clear her head.

New Orleans had a way of embracing the night. The vibrant city streets, with their mix of music and laughter, felt like a different world compared to the quiet solitude of her apartment. She walked through the French Quarter, her senses alive with the sounds and smells of the bustling nightlife. Yet, despite the lively surroundings, she couldn't shake the feeling of being watched.

As she turned down a quieter street, she heard footsteps behind her, quick and purposeful.

Her heart raced, and she quickened her pace, but the footsteps only grew louder. Panic started to set in, but just as she was about to break into a run, a hand grabbed her arm and pulled her into a dark alley.

Elara struggled, but her assailant's grip was too strong. She looked up, expecting to see a mugger or worse, but was met with the intense gaze of the same man from the bookstore.

"It's you," she gasped, fear and confusion mixing in her voice.

"Yes, Elara. It's me," he replied, his voice calm but urgent. "My name is Marcus. I'm here to protect you."

"Protect me?" Elara's head spun with questions. "From what? Who are you really?"

Marcus glanced around, his eyes scanning the dark alley. "There's no time to explain everything right now. You're in danger, Elara. We need to get out of here."

Before she could protest, Marcus lifted her effortlessly, his speed and strength taking her breath away. They moved through the shadows, faster than any human should be able to. Within moments, they were out of the city center and into the outskirts, near the old, abandoned part of town.

He set her down gently, and she stumbled, trying to regain her balance. "What... what are you?" she stammered.

"A friend," he replied, looking into her eyes with a sincerity that was hard to doubt. "And something more. I'm a vampire."

Elara's world tilted on its axis. "A vampire? This can't be real."

"It's real, Elara. And so are you," Marcus said softly. "You are not just human. You are the key to an ancient prophecy. A half-vampire, with powers that neither humans nor vampires fully understand."

Elara shook her head, trying to process the information. "This is insane. Why should I believe you?"

Marcus reached into his coat and pulled out a small, ornate box. He opened it to reveal a shimmering amulet, its center a vibrant red gem that seemed to pulse with its own light. "This belonged to your mother, Elara. She entrusted it to me before she died, knowing one day you would need it."

Tears welled up in Elara's eyes. "My mother... she died when I was a baby. I never knew her."

"And she loved you more than anything," Marcus said gently. "She sacrificed everything to keep you safe. This amulet is part of your legacy. It will help you unlock your true potential."

Elara reached out, her fingers trembling as she touched the amulet. A warmth spread through her hand, up her arm, and into her heart. It was as if she could feel her mother's presence, a comforting and familiar embrace.

"We have to go," Marcus said, his tone urgent again. "Alistair's followers are close. They won't stop until they have you."

"Who is Alistair?" Elara asked, clutching the amulet.

"An ancient and powerful vampire lord," Marcus explained. "He believes in vampire supremacy and will stop at nothing to achieve his goals. You are the key to his plans, but also to stopping him."

Elara took a deep breath, feeling the weight of her new reality settling in. "What do I need to do?"

"First, we need to find a safe place," Marcus said. "Then, we'll train. You need to learn how to harness your powers if we have any chance of stopping Alistair."

With a final look at the city, she once knew, Elara nodded, determination replacing her fear. "Let's go."

Chapter 3
A New Ally

Elara followed Marcus through the labyrinthine streets, her mind racing with everything she had just learned. They moved swiftly and silently, eventually arriving at an inconspicuous brownstone tucked away in a quiet corner of the city. Marcus led her inside, locking the door behind them with a sense of urgency.

The interior of the brownstone was a stark contrast to its exterior. It was filled with ancient artifacts, bookshelves crammed with volumes of history and lore, and the faint scent of incense lingered in the air. Marcus motioned for her to sit on a worn leather couch while he disappeared into another room.

Elara's eyes roamed the space, taking in the rich tapestry of history that surrounded her. She was lost in thought when Marcus returned, accompanied by a young woman with short, curly hair and a pair of glasses perched on her nose. The woman exuded an air of intelligence and confidence.

"Elara, this is Lydia," Marcus introduced her. "She's a member of the Veil and an expert in ancient lore. She's been helping me piece together the prophecy and how it relates to you."

Lydia smiled warmly, extending her hand. "It's a pleasure to meet you, Elara. I've heard a lot about you."

Elara shook Lydia's hand, feeling a sense of relief wash over her. "Nice to meet you too. I guess you know more about me than I do."

"We'll change that soon enough," Lydia replied, her eyes sparkling with enthusiasm. "But first, we need to make sure you're safe. Alistair's followers won't rest until they find you."

Marcus nodded in agreement. "We have a lot of ground to cover. Lydia, can you start by explaining the prophecy in detail?"

Lydia retrieved a thick, ancient book from one of the shelves and laid it on the table. "The prophecy speaks of a Bloodline of Eternity, a lineage that bridges the gap between humans and vampires. It foretells the birth of a half-vampire who possesses the power to either save or destroy both species."

Elara listened intently as Lydia continued, "You are that half-vampire, Elara. Your unique heritage grants you abilities beyond what either species can achieve alone. The amulet you carry is a key, designed to help you unlock and control these powers."

Elara glanced at the amulet around her neck, feeling its comforting warmth. "So, what do I need to do?"

"Training," Marcus interjected. "You need to learn how to harness your abilities and use them effectively. The Veil can provide a safe place for you to train, but we need to move quickly."

Lydia nodded. "There's an old mansion on the outskirts of the city, hidden from prying eyes. It's been used as a safe house for centuries. We can take you there tonight."

Elara took a deep breath, the weight of her destiny pressing down on her. "I'm ready."

As night fell, the three of them made their way to the mansion. The journey was uneventful, but the air was thick with tension. The mansion was a sprawling estate, its grandeur masked by the encroaching forest. Inside, it was a blend of old-world elegance and modern practicality, with rooms dedicated to training and research.

Over the next few days, Elara began her training under Marcus's guidance. They started with the basics, learning to control her heightened senses and physical strength. She quickly discovered she was faster and stronger than she had ever imagined, but controlling her newfound abilities was a challenge.

Lydia, meanwhile, delved into the mansion's extensive library, searching for more information on the prophecy and any potential weaknesses in Alistair's plans. Her research was meticulous, and she often stayed up late into the night, poring over ancient texts and scrolls.

One evening, as Elara was practicing her combat skills with Marcus, Lydia burst into the training room, her eyes wide with excitement.

"I found something," she announced, holding up a dusty old book. "A clue about Alistair's next move. There's a ritual he plans to perform, one that could tip the balance of power in his favor."

Marcus's expression grew serious. "What kind of ritual?"

"It's called the Blood Moon Ritual," Lydia explained. "It requires the blood of a half-vampire to be completed. If Alistair succeeds, he'll gain control over both humans and vampires, bending them to his will."

Elara's blood ran cold. "So that's why he's after me."

"Yes," Lydia confirmed. "But we have a chance to stop him. The ritual can only be performed on the night of a blood moon, which gives us a small window to act."

Marcus turned to Elara; his eyes filled with determination. "We need to find out where Alistair plans to conduct the ritual and stop him before it's too late."

Elara nodded, feeling a renewed sense of purpose. "Let's do it."

Chapter 4
Allies and Preparations

As the blood moon approached, Marcus, Lydia, and Elara knew they needed more help to take on Alistair and his followers. The mansion, though secluded and fortified, would not be enough to protect them. They needed allies, and they needed them quickly.

Marcus suggested they reach out to a network of vampires and humans who were sympathetic to their cause. The Veil had many supporters scattered throughout the city and beyond, individuals who believed in coexistence rather than domination.

Their first stop was an underground club in the French Quarter, known only to those in the supernatural community. It was a place where vampires, humans, and other supernatural beings mingled in a delicate balance of power and secrecy. The club's owner, Theo, was a rogue vampire with a reputation for getting things done.

Elara, Marcus, and Lydia entered the dimly lit club, the pulsing beat of the music reverberating through the floor. The atmosphere was charged with a mix of excitement and danger. Elara could feel the eyes of the patrons on her, some curious, others wary.

Theo stood at the bar, his easy smile not quite reaching his eyes. He was tall and lean, with an air of charm that masked a deep well of secrets. He looked up as they approached, his expression turning serious when he saw Marcus.

"Marcus, it's been a while," Theo greeted, extending a hand.

Marcus shook it firmly. "We need your help, Theo. Alistair's making his move, and we don't have much time."

Theo's eyes flicked to Elara, assessing her with a keen interest. "This must be the famous half-vampire I've been hearing about. Elara, right?"

Elara nodded, trying to appear more confident than she felt. "Yes, that's me."

Theo's smile returned; this time more genuine. "Well, any friend of Marcus is a friend of mine. What do you need?"

Lydia stepped forward, her voice steady and authoritative. "We need allies, and we need information. Alistair is planning to perform the Blood Moon Ritual, and we have to stop him."

Theo's expression darkened. "The Blood Moon Ritual... that's serious. Alistair won't be easy to take down. But I have contacts who might be willing to join the fight. I'll reach out to them."

"Thank you, Theo," Marcus said, his relief palpable.

Theo nodded. "Meet me here tomorrow night. I'll see what I can gather."

As they left the club, Elara felt a glimmer of hope. They were not alone in this fight. With Theo's help, they had a chance to build a resistance strong enough to confront Alistair.

Back at the mansion, the team intensified their preparations. Marcus pushed Elara harder in their training sessions, helping her hone her abilities and learn new techniques. She practiced using the amulet, discovering its power to enhance her strength and agility.

Lydia continued her research, finding more details about the Blood Moon Ritual and possible ways to disrupt it. She also worked on fortifying the mansion, setting up wards and defenses to protect them from any surprise attacks.

As the days passed, Theo arrived with more allies—vampires and humans alike—each with their own skills and resources. There was Jax, a former soldier turned vampire, whose combat expertise was invaluable. Selena, a human witch with knowledge of ancient spells, helped Lydia strengthen their magical defenses. And Gabriel, a vampire with a vast network of spies, provided crucial intelligence on Alistair's movements.

Together, they formed a diverse and formidable team, united by a common goal. They spent hours strategizing, planning their assault on Alistair's stronghold. The tension was high, but so was the sense of camaraderie. Elara felt a growing bond with her new allies, each of them willing to risk everything to stop Alistair.

One evening, as they gathered around the mansion's grand dining table, Lydia unveiled a detailed map of the city, marking potential locations where Alistair might perform the ritual.

"Based on my research and Gabriel's intel, we've narrowed it down to three possible sites," Lydia explained. "An abandoned cathedral, a hidden cave system beneath the city, and an old plantation house on the outskirts."

Marcus studied the map, his brow furrowed. "We'll need to scout each location and look for signs of Alistair's presence. We can't afford to miss anything."

Theo nodded in agreement. "I'll take my team to the cathedral. It's the most exposed, so we'll need to move carefully."

"I'll handle the cave system," Jax volunteered. "It's dangerous, but I've dealt with worse."

Elara felt a surge of determination. "I'll go with Marcus to the plantation house. If Alistair is there, we'll need all the help we can get."

Lydia smiled at her; pride evident in her eyes. "You're ready for this, Elara. We all are. Let's make sure Alistair doesn't succeed."

With their plan in place, the team prepared for their respective missions. The night of the blood moon was fast approaching, and time was running out. Elara knew that the coming days would test them all, but she also knew that together, they had the strength to face whatever lay ahead.

Chapter 5
Scouting the Strongholds

The following night, the team set out to investigate the potential locations for Alistair's ritual. They moved under the cover of darkness, each group taking a different route to their assigned site. Elara and Marcus headed to the old plantation house on the outskirts of the city, their hearts pounding with anticipation and fear.

The plantation house loomed in the distance, its grand facade a ghostly silhouette against the night sky. Overgrown vines and moss clung to the decaying walls, and the once-majestic structure now stood in eerie silence. Elara and Marcus approached cautiously; their senses heightened for any sign of danger.

"We need to be careful," Marcus whispered, his eyes scanning the surroundings. "Alistair's followers could be anywhere."

Elara nodded, gripping the amulet around her neck for reassurance. "Let's stick together and move quickly."

They crept towards the entrance, the wooden door creaking ominously as they pushed it open. Inside, the air was thick with dust and the scent of decay. Broken furniture and tattered curtains added to the atmosphere of neglect, but it was the strange symbols etched into the walls that caught their attention.

"These markings," Elara said, tracing one with her finger. "They look like the ones in the book Lydia showed us."

Marcus examined the symbols closely. "They're part of the ritual. Alistair must have started preparations here. We need to find more evidence."

They moved deeper into the house, their footsteps echoing in the empty halls. In the main hall, they found an altar set up with dark candles and ancient tomes. The sight sent a shiver down Elara's spine.

"This is it," she whispered. "He's planning to perform the ritual here."

Marcus nodded grimly. "We need to get back and inform the others. If we can disrupt his preparations, we might have a chance to stop him."

As they turned to leave, a sudden noise froze them in their tracks. Shadows moved in the corners of the room, and a group of Alistair's followers emerged, their eyes glowing with malevolent intent.

"Intruders," one of them hissed, drawing a blade. "Kill them."

Marcus and Elara sprang into action. Marcus's vampire strength and speed made him a formidable opponent, while Elara, empowered by her amulet, fought with a newfound ferocity. They moved as a team, their movements synchronized and precise.

Despite their skills, the number of attackers was overwhelming. Just as Elara began to tire, a blast of energy knocked the followers back, sending them sprawling. Lydia stood in the doorway, her hands glowing with magical energy.

"We need to go, now!" she shouted, her voice urgent.

Elara and Marcus didn't hesitate. They fought their way through the remaining followers and fled the plantation house, Lydia covering their retreat with powerful spells. Once outside, they ran into the night, not stopping until they reached the safety of the mansion.

Back at the mansion, the atmosphere was tense but focused. Theo, Jax, and the others had returned from their scouting missions with important information. The cathedral and the cave system had shown signs of activity, but nothing as conclusive as what Elara and Marcus had found.

"The plantation house is definitely where Alistair plans to perform the ritual," Marcus announced to the gathered team. "We found the altar and the ritual markings. He's already started the preparations."

"We don't have much time," Lydia added. "The blood moon is only two nights away. We need to strike now, while we still have the element of surprise."

Theo stepped forward; his expression serious. "We'll need a multi-pronged attack. Marcus, Elara, and I will lead the main assault on the plantation house. Jax, you take a team to secure the perimeter and ensure no reinforcements can reach Alistair."

Selena, the witch, spoke up. "I'll set up protective wards around the mansion and provide magical support. We can't afford any distractions."

Gabriel nodded. "I'll use my network to keep an eye on Alistair's movements. If anything changes, you'll know immediately."

The team spent the next hours preparing for the assault. Weapons were sharpened, spells were memorized, and strategies were finalized. Elara felt a mixture of fear and determination as she readied herself for the battle ahead. She knew that the fate of both humans and vampires rested on their success.

As the night of the blood moon approached, the team gathered one last time. Marcus addressed them, his voice filled with resolve.

"This is it. Alistair won't stop until he's achieved his goal, but neither will we. We fight for our future, for a world where humans and vampires can coexist. Let's show him what we're made of."

With a unified sense of purpose, the team set out into the night, ready to face the greatest challenge of their lives. The blood moon began to rise, casting an eerie red glow over the city. The final confrontation was about to begin.

Chapter 6
The Battle of the Blood Moon

The blood moon hung ominously in the sky, casting its crimson glow over the city as the team approached the plantation house. The tension in the air was palpable, each step heavy with the anticipation of the impending battle. Elara felt her heart pounding, but the presence of her allies gave her strength. She knew they were ready to face whatever lay ahead.

Marcus led the way, his movements swift and silent. Theo and Lydia flanked Elara, their eyes scanning the surroundings for any sign of danger. Jax and his team spread out to secure the perimeter, ensuring no one could escape or call for reinforcements.

As they neared the entrance, Marcus held up a hand, signaling them to stop. He motioned for Lydia, who began to mutter an incantation under her breath. A faint shimmer appeared in the air, revealing the hidden wards protecting the house.

"These wards are strong," Lydia whispered. "It'll take me a moment to break through them."

Elara watched as Lydia worked her magic, her hands glowing with energy. She could see the strain on Lydia's face, but the witch's determination never wavered. Finally, the wards flickered and vanished, allowing them to proceed.

"Let's move," Marcus said, his voice a low growl.

They entered the house, the air thick with the scent of incense and dark magic. The ritual markings on the walls seemed to pulse with an otherworldly energy. As they moved deeper into the house, the sounds of chanting grew louder.

They reached the main hall, where Alistair stood at the center of the ritual circle, his followers gathered around him. The vampire lord's eyes glowed with a sinister light as he held a dagger above the altar, ready to begin the ritual.

"Alistair!" Marcus shouted, his voice echoing through the chamber. "It's over. We're here to stop you."

Alistair turned slowly, a cruel smile spreading across his face. "Ah, Marcus. How predictable. And you brought the girl. Perfect."

Elara felt a surge of anger at his words. She stepped forward, her voice steady. "You're not going to win, Alistair. We'll stop you, no matter what it takes."

Alistair laughed, a cold, chilling sound. "You think you can stop me? The power of the Blood Moon will make me unstoppable. But if you insist on dying, then so be it."

He raised his hand, and his followers surged forward, attacking with a frenzy. The room erupted into chaos as the battle began. Marcus and Theo fought side by side, their movements a blur of speed and strength. Lydia cast spells to protect their allies and disrupt Alistair's magic, while Jax and his team battled fiercely at the entrance to keep reinforcements at bay.

Elara found herself face to face with Alistair, the amulet around her neck glowing with power. She could feel its energy coursing through her, giving her strength and clarity. She knew this was her moment, her chance to fulfill her destiny.

Alistair lunged at her; his dagger aimed for her heart. Elara dodged and countered with a swift strike, the amulet's power enhancing her movements. Their battle was intense, each strike met with a counter, each blow more ferocious than the last.

"You're strong, but not strong enough," Alistair taunted, his eyes blazing.

Elara gritted her teeth, focusing on the amulet's power. She remembered her mother's sacrifice, Marcus's teachings, and the support of her allies. She couldn't fail.

With a burst of energy, Elara unleashed the full power of the amulet. A wave of light erupted from her, knocking Alistair back and disrupting the ritual. The dagger flew from his hand, landing harmlessly on the floor.

Alistair roared in fury, but before he could recover, Marcus and Theo were upon him. They fought with a ferocity born of years of training and a determination to protect what they held dear. Finally, Marcus landed a decisive blow, incapacitating Alistair and bringing him to his knees.

Elara approached, her breath coming in ragged gasps. She looked down at the defeated vampire lord, her voice steady and resolute. "It's over, Alistair. You'll never hurt anyone again."

With a final, powerful incantation from Lydia, the ritual circle shattered, its dark energy dissipating into the air. The battle was won, but the cost had been high. The team surveyed the aftermath, their faces marked with exhaustion and relief.

As dawn broke, the blood moon faded, and the first rays of sunlight pierced the gloom. The team regrouped outside the plantation house; their spirits buoyed by their victory.

Marcus placed a hand on Elara's shoulder, pride shining in his eyes. "You did it, Elara. You stopped him."

Elara smiled, feeling a deep sense of accomplishment. "We did it, together."

Theo approached; his usual carefree demeanor replaced by genuine respect. "You were incredible out there. We couldn't have done it without you."

Lydia joined them, her face glowing with pride. "The prophecy was right. You are the key to our future, Elara."

Elara looked at her friends, her heart swelling with gratitude and determination. They had faced the darkness together and emerged victorious. Now, they could look forward to a future where humans and vampires could coexist in peace.

As they walked away from the plantation house, Elara knew that this was just the beginning. There were still challenges ahead, but with her friends by her side, she was ready to face whatever came next.

Chapter 7
A New Dawn

As the first light of dawn broke over the horizon, Elara, Marcus, Lydia, Theo, and the rest of their allies made their way back to the mansion. The battle had taken its toll, but their spirits were high with the satisfaction of victory. The threat of Alistair's domination had been thwarted, and they had proven that unity and determination could overcome even the darkest forces.

The mansion, once a place of secrecy and preparation, now felt like a sanctuary. They gathered in the grand dining room, where the sunlight filtered through the windows, casting a warm glow on their faces. Elara looked around at her friends and allies, feeling a profound sense of gratitude for each of them.

Marcus stood at the head of the table; his expression serious but hopeful. "Last night, we faced a great evil and emerged victorious.

But our work is not done. We must ensure that the balance between humans and vampires is maintained and that the peace we fought for endures."

Lydia nodded, her eyes shining with determination. "We have a chance to build a better future, one where our two worlds can coexist. We must take this opportunity to strengthen the Veil and protect both species."

Theo leaned back in his chair, a playful smile on his lips. "And we need to celebrate our victory. We earned it."

The room filled with laughter, a welcome relief after the intensity of the battle. They spent the morning sharing stories, making plans, and enjoying each other's company. The bond they had formed was strong, and they knew that together, they could face any challenge.

Later that day, Elara and Marcus took a walk in the mansion's garden. The air was fresh and filled with the scent of blooming flowers. Elara felt a sense of peace she hadn't known in a long time.

"How are you feeling?" Marcus asked, his voice gentle.

Elara smiled, looking up at the sky. "Tired, but hopeful. We did something incredible, didn't we?"

Marcus nodded, his eyes reflecting the same hope. "Yes, we did. And it's only the beginning. There's so much more to do, but I know we can handle it."

Elara took a deep breath, feeling the weight of her destiny lift slightly. "Thank you, Marcus. For everything. I couldn't have done this without you."

Marcus shook his head, his expression serious. "You were the key, Elara. Your strength and courage inspired all of us. Your mother would be proud."

Tears welled up in Elara's eyes, but they were tears of joy and relief. She felt her mother's presence, a comforting warmth that reassured her she was on the right path.

In the following weeks, the Veil convened to discuss their plans for the future. Representatives from various factions, both human and vampire, gathered to ensure that the fragile peace was maintained and strengthened.

Elara stood before them, her voice clear and confident. "We have shown that humans and vampires can work together, that we can overcome our differences for the greater good. We must continue to build on this foundation, to create a world where our children can live without fear."

The leaders of the Veil nodded in agreement, their support bolstering her resolve. They discussed new policies, ways to integrate their communities, and strategies to protect against future threats. The road ahead was long, but the spirit of cooperation and mutual respect gave them hope.

Despite the busy days, Elara made time for herself, exploring her powers and learning more about her heritage. She visited her mother's grave, the amulet glowing softly in her hand.

"I wish you were here to see this," she whispered, feeling a connection that transcended time and space. "But I know you're watching over me. I promise to honor your memory and make you proud."

She placed the amulet on the grave, feeling a surge of energy and love. It was a reminder of her past, but also a symbol of the future she was determined to build.

To mark their victory and the beginning of a new era, the Veil organized a grand celebration. The mansion was transformed into a place of joy and festivity, with music, dancing, and laughter filling the air.

Elara moved through the crowd, greeting friends and allies, her heart light with happiness. She found Marcus and Lydia near the dance floor, their faces glowing with the joy of the moment.

"Come on, Elara," Lydia called, pulling her onto the dance floor. "It's time to celebrate!"

Elara laughed, joining in the dance, feeling a sense of freedom and exhilaration. As the music played and the night wore on, she knew that they had achieved something extraordinary. They had faced the darkness and emerged stronger, united by a common purpose.

Months passed, and the peace they had fought for held strong. The Veil continued its work, ensuring that humans and vampires could coexist in harmony. Elara, Marcus, Lydia, Theo, and their allies remained vigilant, ready to face any new challenges that arose.

Elara stood at the edge of the city, looking out at the horizon. The sun was setting, casting a golden glow over the landscape. She felt a sense of contentment and purpose, knowing that they had created a better world.

As the first stars appeared in the sky, Elara turned and walked back toward the city, her heart filled with hope. She knew that the journey was far from over, but with her friends by her side, she was ready for whatever came next.

Chapter 8
Shadows and Light

The months of peace following their victory over Alistair had brought a sense of stability and hope, but the world of humans and vampires was ever-changing. Elara and her allies remained vigilant, knowing that new challenges could arise at any moment.

The Veil's headquarters, once a place shrouded in secrecy, had become a bustling center of activity. Representatives from various factions worked together, their combined efforts focused on maintaining the fragile peace and addressing any threats that emerged.

Elara, now a respected leader within the Veil, sat at a large table with Marcus, Lydia, Theo, and other key members of the council. Maps and documents were spread out before them, detailing recent incidents and areas of concern.

Lydia pointed to a map; her brow furrowed. "We've been getting reports of increased activity in the northern regions. It seems like rogue vampire groups are trying to take advantage of the power vacuum left by Alistair's defeat."

Marcus nodded. "We need to address this before it becomes a larger issue. If these groups unite, they could pose a serious threat."

Theo leaned back in his chair; his eyes thoughtful. "We should send a team to investigate and establish a presence there. Show them that the Veil is still strong and won't tolerate any attempts to disrupt the peace."

Elara agreed, her mind already working on a plan. "I'll lead the team. We need to show that our commitment to peace and cooperation is unwavering."

The council members nodded in agreement, their trust in Elara evident. "We'll support you in any way we can," Lydia said, her voice firm.

Elara and her chosen team prepared for their journey to the northern regions. Marcus, Theo, Jax, and Selena volunteered to accompany her, each bringing their unique skills to the mission. They gathered supplies, weapons, and information, ensuring they were ready for whatever lay ahead.

As they packed, Elara took a moment to speak with Marcus privately. "Do you think we're doing the right thing, Marcus? Going out there, facing new threats?"

Marcus smiled; his eyes warm with reassurance. "Absolutely. We fought for this peace, and now we need to protect it. Together, we can handle anything that comes our way."

Elara felt a surge of gratitude and determination. "Thank you, Marcus. Your faith means a lot to me."

The journey to the northern regions was long and arduous. The landscape grew harsher, the air colder, as they traveled further from the safety of the city. They moved cautiously, aware that danger could be lurking around every corner.

One evening, as they set up camp, Theo returned from scouting with a grim expression. "We've found traces of a large group of vampires nearby. They seem to be gathering in an old fortress a few miles from here."

Jax tightened his grip on his weapon. "Sounds like they're planning something big. We need to act fast."

Selena nodded, her magical senses alert. "I can sense a lot of dark energy in that area. We should be prepared for anything."

Elara took a deep breath, steeling herself for the challenge ahead. "We'll approach carefully, gather as much information as we can, and then decide on the best course of action."

As night fell, they moved towards the fortress, their movements silent and deliberate. The fortress loomed ahead, its dark silhouette a stark contrast against the starry sky. They could see the flicker of torches and hear the murmur of voices, confirming Theo's report.

Sneaking inside the fortress, they observed the gathering from the shadows. Dozens of vampires, led by a charismatic and ruthless leader named Viktor, were discussing their plans to challenge the Veil and seize control of the region.

Viktor's voice echoed through the chamber, his tone commanding. "The Veil is weak, fragmented. This is our chance to rise and claim what is rightfully ours. We will not bow to their rules any longer."

Elara felt a chill run down her spine. Viktor's words were met with cheers and applause from the gathered vampires, their loyalty and determination evident.

Marcus leaned in, his voice a whisper. "We need to disrupt this meeting and show them that the Veil is not weak. If we can take down Viktor, the rest might back off."

Elara nodded, formulating a plan. "We'll strike swiftly and decisively. Selena, use your magic to create a distraction. Theo, Jax, and Marcus, take out the key guards. I'll go after Viktor."

They moved into position, each taking a deep breath as they prepared for the attack. Selena's hands glowed with magical energy, and with a flick of her wrist, she sent a wave of illusions and bright lights into the chamber, causing chaos and confusion among Viktor's followers.

As the vampires scrambled to understand what was happening, Theo, Jax, and Marcus moved with deadly precision, neutralizing the guards and clearing a path for Elara. She darted towards Viktor, her movements swift and purposeful.

Viktor turned, his eyes narrowing as he saw her approach. "So, the half-vampire thinks she can stop me? You're a fool."

Elara met his gaze, her voice steady. "No, Viktor. You're the fool if you think you can disrupt the peace we've fought for."

Their battle was intense, a clash of strength and skill. Viktor was powerful, but Elara's training and the amulet's power gave her the edge. With a final, decisive strike, she disarmed Viktor and pinned him to the ground.

"Yield," Elara commanded, her voice firm.

Viktor sneered, but the fight had drained him. "Fine. You win this time, but this isn't over."

Elara tightened her grip, her eyes blazing. "It is for now. Take your followers and leave. If you ever threaten the peace again, we won't be so merciful."

With Viktor subdued, the rest of his followers quickly dispersed, their morale shattered. The team regrouped; their victory hard-earned but complete.

The journey back to the mansion was filled with a sense of accomplishment and relief. They had faced a new threat and emerged victorious, proving once again that unity and determination could overcome any challenge.

As they entered the mansion, they were greeted with cheers and applause from their allies. The news of their victory had spread quickly, bolstering the morale of the Veil and reaffirming their commitment to peace.

Elara stood before her friends and allies; her heart filled with pride. "We did it. We've shown that the Veil is strong and that we will protect this peace with everything we have. Thank you, all of you, for your courage and dedication."

Marcus stepped forward, placing a hand on her shoulder. "You've proven yourself as a true leader, Elara. We couldn't have done this without you."

Lydia smiled, her eyes shining with pride. "Here's to many more victories and a future filled with hope."

As they celebrated their success, Elara knew that the journey was far from over. But with her friends by her side and the strength of the Veil behind her, she was ready to face whatever came next. The shadows of the past had been defeated, and the light of a new dawn was rising.

Bloodlines of Eternity

Chapter 9
Whispers of the Past

In the weeks following their victory over Viktor, life began to settle into a new rhythm. The Veil continued its work, maintaining peace and strengthening alliances. Elara found herself growing more comfortable in her role as a leader, her confidence bolstered by the support of her friends and allies.

One evening, Elara sat in the mansion's library, poring over ancient texts and scrolls. She had developed a fascination with the history of vampires and humans, seeking to understand the complexities of their intertwined destinies. As she read, she stumbled upon a reference to a legendary artifact known as the Shadow Key, said to hold the power to unlock secrets of the past.

Intrigued, Elara called for Lydia and Marcus to join her. "I found something interesting," she said, pointing to the passage in the book. "The Shadow Key. Have you heard of it?"

Lydia's eyes widened as she read the passage. "The Shadow Key is a myth, said to reveal hidden truths and unlock forgotten memories. If it exists, it could provide invaluable insight into our history and perhaps even our future."

Marcus leaned over the book; his expression thoughtful. "It's worth investigating. If the Shadow Key can help us understand more about our heritage and the prophecy, we should find it."

Elara nodded, feeling a sense of excitement. "Let's gather the team and start looking for clues."

The team, now including Theo, Jax, and Selena, assembled to discuss their new quest. They decided to start their search in the city archives, hoping to find any references or clues about the Shadow Key's location.

The archives were a treasure trove of historical documents, maps, and records. As they sifted through the dusty files, Elara stumbled upon an old map that showed a hidden cave system beneath the city, rumored to be a resting place for ancient artifacts.

"This could be it," she said, showing the map to the others. "The caves might hold the key we're looking for."

Theo grinned, his eyes sparkling with excitement. "An underground adventure? Count me in."

Jax nodded, his expression serious. "We should be cautious. If the Shadow Key is real, we won't be the only ones looking for it."

Selena added, "I'll prepare some protective spells. We don't know what we'll find down there."

With their plan in place, they set out for the caves the next morning, their hearts filled with anticipation and a sense of adventure.

The entrance to the cave system was hidden behind an overgrown thicket, the opening barely visible in the dim light. As they descended into the darkness, the air grew cool and damp, the sounds of the city fading away to be replaced by the echoing drip of water and the rustle of unseen creatures.

Lydia led the way, her magical light illuminating the path ahead. "Stay close and keep your eyes open. These caves have been untouched for centuries."

As they ventured deeper, the tunnels became narrower and more labyrinthine. Strange symbols and markings on the walls hinted at the ancient inhabitants of the caves, their meanings long forgotten.

After hours of navigating the maze-like passages, they reached a large cavern. In the center of the cavern stood a pedestal, and atop it rested a small, intricately carved box.

"Could this be it?" Theo asked, his voice a whisper.

Elara approached the pedestal cautiously, her heart pounding. She reached out and opened the box, revealing a gleaming, black key—the Shadow Key.

"It's real," she breathed, holding the key up to the light.

Suddenly, a low growl echoed through the cavern, and shadows shifted around them. A group of rogue vampires emerged from the darkness; their eyes fixed on the key.

"Hand it over," their leader snarled, his fangs bared. "The Shadow Key belongs to us."

Marcus stepped forward; his stance protective. "You'll have to get through us first."

The battle that ensued was fierce and chaotic. Elara, Marcus, and the others fought with all their strength, determined to protect the key. Selena's spells lit up the cavern, creating barriers and blasting their attackers with bursts of energy.

In the midst of the fight, Elara felt a surge of power from the amulet. She focused on the key, willing its energy to help them. A wave of dark energy emanated from the key, disorienting their enemies and giving her allies the upper hand.

With the rogue vampires defeated, the team regrouped, breathing heavily but victorious. Elara held the Shadow Key tightly, feeling its power and significance.

"Let's get out of here," Marcus said, his voice steady. "We need to study this key and find out what secrets it holds."

Back at the mansion, Lydia began examining the Shadow Key, using her knowledge of ancient lore and magic to unlock its secrets. As she worked, Elara and Marcus watched, their anticipation growing.

Finally, Lydia looked up, her eyes filled with wonder. "The key is connected to an ancient vault, hidden deep within the mountains. It contains the memories and knowledge of our ancestors, preserved for those who are worthy to find it."

Elara felt a thrill of excitement. "We need to find this vault. It could hold the answers to so many questions."

Marcus nodded; his expression determined. "Then we start planning our next journey. This is just the beginning."

With the discovery of the Shadow Key, the team prepared for their journey to the mountains where the ancient vault was hidden. The prospect of uncovering the secrets of their ancestors filled them with anticipation and a renewed sense of purpose.

The mansion buzzed with activity as the team gathered supplies and planned their route to the mountains. Maps were spread out on the large dining table, alongside equipment and provisions for the journey.

Elara, Marcus, Lydia, Theo, Jax, and Selena were all present, each focused on their tasks. Elara felt a sense of camaraderie and determination among them.

"We need to be prepared for anything," Marcus said, looking around at his friends. "This journey will be dangerous, but it's crucial. The knowledge in that vault could change everything."

Lydia nodded; her eyes bright with excitement. "I've enchanted our gear to provide additional protection. The mountains are treacherous, and who knows what guardians might be protecting the vault."

Theo grinned, his usual charm shining through. "Sounds like an adventure. Let's make sure we're ready for whatever comes our way."

The team set out at dawn, leaving the city behind as they headed towards the distant mountains. The landscape gradually changed from urban sprawl to rolling hills and dense forests. The air grew colder and crisper as they ascended, the path becoming more rugged and challenging.

They traveled for days, facing various obstacles and trials along the way. Crossing rivers, navigating through dense forests, and climbing steep inclines tested their endurance and teamwork.

One evening, as they set up camp under the stars, Elara sat by the fire, reflecting on their journey. Marcus joined her, his presence a comforting anchor.

"How are you holding up?" he asked, his voice gentle.

Elara smiled, looking into the fire. "I'm good. This journey... it's hard, but it feels right. Like we're on the path we were meant to take."

Marcus nodded; his gaze thoughtful. "We're making history, Elara. Whatever we find in that vault, it will be because of your leadership and determination."

Elara felt a warmth in her heart at his words. "And because of our teamwork. I couldn't do this without all of you."

As they approached the base of the mountains, the terrain became even more challenging. They climbed steep cliffs, crossed narrow ledges, and braved icy winds. The higher they went, the more treacherous the path became.

One day, as they were navigating a particularly difficult ascent, a sudden rockslide caught them off guard. Boulders tumbled down the mountainside, threatening to sweep them away.

"Watch out!" Jax shouted, pushing Lydia out of the path of a falling rock.

Elara and Marcus scrambled to find cover, their hearts pounding. Selena raised her hands, casting a protective spell that deflected some of the debris, but the situation was dire.

Theo, using his agility and quick thinking, found a small alcove in the rock face. "Over here!" he called, helping the others to safety.

As the dust settled, they assessed their situation. No one was seriously injured, but the path ahead was blocked.

"We need to find another way," Marcus said, his voice steady. "The rockslide has made this route impassable."

Lydia consulted the map, her brow furrowed. "There's an alternate path, but it's longer and more difficult. We'll need to be extra careful."

With renewed determination, they set off on the new path, their spirits undaunted. They were close to their goal, and nothing would stop them now.

After days of arduous climbing, they finally reached a secluded plateau near the mountain's peak. Before them stood a massive stone door, engraved with intricate symbols and runes.

"This must be it," Elara said, her voice filled with awe. "The entrance to the vault."

Lydia stepped forward, examining the door. "The symbols... they match the ones on the Shadow Key. I think the key is the way to open it."

Elara took the Shadow Key from her pack, feeling its power resonate in her hand. She approached the door, fitting the key into a central lock. As she turned it, the runes glowed with a soft light, and the door began to rumble open.

Inside, the vault was a vast, echoing chamber filled with ancient artifacts, scrolls, and books. The air was thick with the scent of old parchment and the faint hum of magic.

As they ventured deeper into the vault, they discovered a central altar adorned with a large, ornate tome. Lydia carefully opened the tome, her eyes widening as she read its contents.

"This is incredible," she whispered. "It contains the history of our ancestors, their knowledge, their secrets. Everything we've been searching for."

Elara felt a surge of excitement and reverence. "This is what we've been looking for. The key to understanding our past and shaping our future."

They spent hours exploring the vault, each discovery more astounding than the last. They found records of ancient prophecies, descriptions of powerful artifacts, and detailed accounts of the early days of the Veil.

As they pieced together the information, a clearer picture of their heritage and destiny emerged. They realized that their journey was just beginning and that they had a responsibility to use this knowledge to protect and guide both humans and vampires.

With their newfound knowledge, the team made their way back down the mountain. The journey was still challenging, but their spirits were high, buoyed by their discoveries.

When they finally returned to the mansion, they were greeted with awe and admiration. The information and artifacts they brought back would change the course of history and strengthen the Veil's mission.

Elara stood before her friends and allies, holding the Shadow Key. "We've unlocked the secrets of our past and found the guidance we need for the future. Together, we'll build a world where humans and vampires can coexist in peace and harmony."

The room erupted in cheers, and Elara felt a deep sense of fulfillment and purpose. They had faced great challenges and emerged stronger, united by their shared vision and determination.

Chapter 11
Uniting the Clans

The weeks following their return from the vault were filled with activity and excitement. The knowledge and artifacts they had uncovered provided invaluable insights into their heritage and the early days of the Veil. But with this newfound power came new responsibilities. Elara and her allies knew they needed to strengthen alliances and unite the vampire clans to ensure lasting peace.

Elara stood at the head of the table in the Veil's headquarters, her voice confident and resolute. "We have an unprecedented opportunity to bring the vampire clans together. The knowledge we've gained from the vault can help us forge a united front, but we need to act quickly and decisively."

Lydia spread a map on the table, marking the locations of various vampire clans across the region. "I've been reaching out to our contacts. Some clans are open to negotiation, but others are wary of the Veil and our intentions."

Marcus nodded. "We need to show them that unity is in everyone's best interest. We should start with the influential clans and work our way down."

Theo leaned forward; his eyes gleaming with enthusiasm. "I'll take care of the more... skeptical clans. They might need a bit more convincing, but I'm up for the challenge."

Elara smiled, grateful for her friends' support. "We'll divide and conquer. Lydia, continue your research and prepare any historical evidence that might help persuade the clans. Marcus, Theo, and I will visit the key clans and start negotiations."

Their first stop was the Crimson Moon clan, known for their warrior traditions and fierce independence. Elara, Marcus, and Theo arrived at their stronghold, a fortified mansion deep in the forest. They were greeted with suspicion, but the presence of Marcus, a respected figure among vampires, helped ease the tension.

Elara addressed the clan's leader, a formidable vampire named Sorin. "We come in peace, seeking to unite our clans for the greater good. The knowledge we've uncovered from the ancient vault can benefit us all."

Sorin studied them, his expression unreadable. "We've heard of your exploits, Elara. But why should we trust the Veil? We've thrived independently for centuries."

Marcus stepped forward, his voice calm and authoritative. "Because the threats we face are greater than any one clan can handle alone. Alistair's defeat was just the beginning. There will be others who seek to disrupt the balance and seize power. United, we stand a better chance of protecting our way of life."

Elara added, "The knowledge we've gained includes strategies and tactics from our ancestors, who faced similar challenges. We can learn from their successes and avoid their mistakes."

Sorin seemed to consider their words, the weight of his clan's history in his eyes. "Very well. We will hear more of what you have to offer. But know this: the Crimson Moon clan will not be swayed easily."

The next stop was the Shadow Hunters, a clan renowned for their stealth and espionage skills. Their leader, a cunning vampire named Natalia, was known for her shrewdness and strategic mind.

Elara and her team arrived at a secluded underground lair, where Natalia awaited them. "So, the Veil seeks our support," she said, her tone skeptical. "What makes you think we need your help?"

Theo, always the charmer, smiled warmly. "Because, Natalia, you understand the value of alliances. The knowledge we offer could enhance your clan's abilities and secure your position in the new order we're trying to establish."

Lydia, who had joined them for this meeting, produced a scroll from the vault. "This document details the espionage techniques of our ancestors. It could greatly enhance your clan's capabilities."

Natalia's eyes gleamed with interest as she examined the scroll. "Interesting. Very well, I'll consider your proposal. But be warned: we value our independence above all else."

Their final stop was the Silver Fang clan, known for their scholars and healers. Their leader, an elderly vampire named Armand, welcomed them with curiosity and open-mindedness.

Elara presented a collection of ancient medical texts and potions from the vault. "These are remedies and techniques from our ancestors, lost to time. With your clan's expertise, we could revive and improve upon them, benefiting all vampires."

Armand studied the texts, his eyes filled with wonder. "This is remarkable. If we could combine this ancient knowledge with our own, it would be a great boon to our people."

Marcus added, "A united front would ensure that this knowledge is preserved and used for the good of all clans."

Armand nodded, a smile spreading across his face. "You have our support. The Silver Fang clan will stand with the Veil."

With the support of key clans secured, Elara and her allies organized a great gathering, inviting representatives from all vampire clans to the Veil's headquarters. The atmosphere was tense but hopeful as leaders and delegates assembled.

Elara addressed the gathering, her voice clear and powerful. "We stand at a crossroads. Our ancestors have shown us the way through the knowledge we've uncovered. United, we can face any challenge and ensure a prosperous future for all vampires."

Lydia presented the ancient documents and artifacts, highlighting the benefits of cooperation and unity. Theo and Marcus shared their experiences, emphasizing the importance of mutual support and trust.

As the gathering progressed, old rivalries and suspicions began to fade, replaced by a sense of shared purpose and vision. The clans discussed, debated, and ultimately agreed to form a council, with representatives from each clan working together under the guidance of the Veil.

The creation of the council marked the beginning of a new era. The clans, united and stronger than ever, began working together to protect their world and ensure peace. Elara felt a deep sense of accomplishment and hope as she stood with her friends and allies.

Marcus placed a hand on her shoulder, his voice filled with pride. "We did it, Elara. We've built something truly remarkable."

Lydia smiled, her eyes shining with happiness. "This is just the beginning. There's so much more we can achieve together."

Theo grinned; his usual charm evident. "To the future, and all the adventures it holds."

Elara looked at her friends, feeling a surge of gratitude and determination. They had faced great challenges and emerged victorious, united by their shared vision and strength. The future was bright, filled with possibilities, and she was ready to face whatever came next with her allies by her side.

Chapter 12
Shadows of Betrayal

With the vampire clans united and a new council established, the future looked bright. However, not everyone was content with the new order. Hidden among the allies and the shadows of their world, a new threat began to emerge—one that could shatter the fragile peace they had worked so hard to achieve.

The first official council meeting was held at the Veil's headquarters. Representatives from each clan sat around the large table, discussing plans for cooperation and mutual protection. Elara presided over the meeting, her leadership and vision guiding the discussions.

Marcus stood to address the council. "Our first priority should be to establish communication channels and protocols for sharing information. This will help us respond quickly to any threats and maintain our united front."

Natalia, the leader of the Shadow Hunters, nodded. "Agreed. My clan can assist with intelligence gathering and covert operations. We have the skills and resources to monitor potential threats."

Armand of the Silver Fang clan added, "We should also focus on education and training. Sharing our knowledge and techniques will strengthen us all."

The council members nodded in agreement, their commitment to unity clear. As the meeting progressed, they outlined plans for joint training exercises, shared resources, and coordinated defense strategies.

After the meeting, Elara walked through the quiet halls of the mansion, reflecting on their progress. She felt a sense of pride and optimism, but also a nagging sense of unease.

As she turned a corner, she heard a faint whisper, like a breeze through the shadows.

"Elara..." The voice was soft and haunting, sending a chill down her spine.

She turned, but saw no one. The mansion was empty, the only sound her own breathing. "Who's there?" she called, her voice steady despite the fear creeping into her heart.

The whisper came again, closer this time. "Beware... betrayal comes from within..."

Elara's heart pounded as she searched the shadows, but found nothing. She knew she couldn't ignore the warning, even if it was just a figment of her imagination.

The next morning, Elara gathered her closest allies—Marcus, Lydia, Theo, Jax, and Selena—in the library. She recounted the eerie whisper she had heard and her growing sense of unease.

"I don't want to alarm anyone, but we need to be vigilant," she said. "Someone or something is trying to undermine us."

Marcus frowned; his expression serious. "We should investigate quietly, without causing panic. If there's a traitor among us, we need to identify them before they can do any damage."

Lydia nodded. "I'll start researching any unusual activity or signs of betrayal. Theo, can you use your connections to gather information discreetly?"

Theo grinned. "Consider it done. I'll see what I can dig up."

Jax and Selena volunteered to increase security around the mansion and keep an eye on the council members. They knew that trust was crucial, but so was caution.

Over the next few days, the team worked tirelessly to uncover any signs of betrayal.

Lydia combed through historical records and magical texts, searching for clues. Theo used his charm and network of contacts to gather information, while Jax and Selena kept watch over the mansion.

One evening, Theo returned with troubling news. "I've heard whispers of a group within the council plotting against us. They're unhappy with the new order and want to seize power for themselves."

Elara's heart sank. "Do you know who they are?"

Theo shook his head. "Not yet, but I'm getting closer. We need to be careful and act quickly."

Marcus placed a reassuring hand on Elara's shoulder. "We'll get through this, just like we have before. We'll find the traitors and stop them."

The team continued their investigation, piecing together the puzzle. They discovered that the traitors were planning to disrupt the next council meeting, using it as an opportunity to seize control and sow chaos.

On the day of the meeting, Elara and her allies prepared for the confrontation. They alerted their trusted council members and set a plan in motion to expose the traitors and prevent their coup.

As the meeting began, Elara addressed the council, her voice steady and commanding. "We've come a long way, but our journey is far from over. We must remain vigilant and united against those who seek to divide us."

Suddenly, a group of council members rose from their seats, their expressions hostile. "You're right, Elara," one of them sneered. "The time for change is now. We will not be ruled by the Veil any longer."

Chaos erupted as the traitors revealed themselves, attacking with the intent to overthrow the council. Elara and her allies sprang into action, fighting to protect their hard-won peace.

The battle was intense, but Elara and her allies fought with determination and skill. Lydia used her magic to shield them from harm, while Jax and Selena fought with ferocity and precision. Marcus and Theo coordinated their efforts, taking down the traitors one by one.

In the midst of the chaos, Elara faced off against the leader of the traitors, a vampire named Darius. He was strong and cunning, but Elara's training and the power of the amulet gave her the upper hand.

"You will not destroy what we've built," Elara said, her voice filled with resolve. "We stand for unity and peace, and we will prevail."

With a final, powerful strike, Elara defeated Darius, ending the battle. The remaining traitors surrendered; their rebellion crushed.

In the aftermath of the battle, the council worked to rebuild trust and strengthen their bonds. The traitors were dealt with justly, and measures were put in place to prevent future betrayals.

Elara stood before the council; her voice filled with hope. "We have faced another challenge and emerged stronger. Let this be a reminder that unity is our greatest strength. Together, we can overcome any obstacle."

The council members nodded in agreement, their commitment to the new order renewed. They knew that the road ahead would be difficult, but they were ready to face it together.

That evening, Elara and Marcus sat in the mansion's garden, the stars shining brightly above them. The air was cool and filled with the scent of blooming flowers.

"We did it," Elara said, a smile playing on her lips. "We stopped the traitors and protected the council."

Marcus nodded, his eyes reflecting the light of the stars. "And we'll continue to protect it, together."

Elara felt a deep sense of contentment and purpose. She knew that there would always be challenges, but with her friends and allies by her side, she was ready to face them.

As the night wore on, Elara and Marcus talked about the future, their hearts filled with hope and determination. The shadows of betrayal had been vanquished, and the light of their vision shone brighter than ever.

Chapter 13
Echoes of the Past

The threat of betrayal had been dealt with, but Elara and her allies knew they could not afford to let their guard down. As they continued to strengthen their alliances and protect their world, a new mystery began to unfold—one that would lead them deep into the history of their ancestors and reveal long-hidden secrets.

One morning, as Elara was sorting through the ancient artifacts they had retrieved from the vault, she came across an old, dusty scroll. Its edges were frayed, and the parchment was brittle with age. Curious, she carefully unrolled it and began to read.

The scroll detailed the existence of a hidden chamber within the vault, containing powerful relics and forgotten knowledge. It spoke of a guardian spirit, bound to protect the chamber and its secrets.

Elara immediately called for Lydia, Marcus, and the others. "Look at this," she said, showing them the scroll. "There's a hidden chamber within the vault, guarded by a spirit. We need to find it."

Lydia's eyes widened as she examined the scroll. "This is incredible. If the chamber exists, it could hold even more valuable information and artifacts."

Marcus nodded. "We should prepare to return to the vault and search for this hidden chamber. It could provide us with the tools we need to face future threats."

With renewed determination, Elara, Marcus, Lydia, Theo, Jax, and Selena set out for the mountains once more. The journey was familiar but no less challenging, the rugged terrain testing their endurance and resolve.

As they arrived at the vault, they were greeted by the same sense of awe and reverence. The ancient structure stood as a testament to their ancestors' wisdom and strength.

They entered the vault and began their search for the hidden chamber. Using the clues from the scroll, they navigated through the labyrinthine passages, their anticipation growing with each step.

After hours of searching, they finally found a concealed door, its surface covered in intricate carvings. The symbols matched those described in the scroll, confirming that they had found the hidden chamber.

Elara placed her hand on the door, feeling a surge of energy. The door slowly opened, revealing a dimly lit chamber filled with ancient relics and tomes. In the center of the room stood a pedestal, atop which rested a glowing crystal.

As they entered the chamber, a ghostly figure materialized before them—a guardian spirit, as described in the scroll. The spirit was an ethereal presence, its form shifting and shimmering in the dim light.

"Who dares enter this sacred chamber?" the spirit intoned, its voice echoing through the room.

Elara stepped forward, her voice steady and respectful. "We are descendants of those who built this vault. We seek the knowledge and relics contained within to protect our world and honor our ancestors."

The spirit regarded them with a penetrating gaze. "To prove your worthiness, you must pass a test. Only then will I allow you to access the chamber's secrets."

The spirit led them to a series of challenges, each designed to test their courage, wisdom, and unity. The first challenge was a test of strength and endurance, requiring them to navigate a treacherous obstacle course.

Jax and Selena took the lead, their physical prowess and agility helping them overcome the obstacles. The rest of the team followed, their determination and teamwork guiding them through the course.

The second challenge was a test of wisdom, involving complex puzzles and riddles. Lydia and Theo worked together, using their knowledge and intellect to solve each puzzle. Elara and Marcus assisted, their combined efforts ensuring success.

The final challenge was a test of unity and trust. They were required to cross a chasm, relying solely on each other to navigate the narrow, unstable path. As they worked together, their bond grew stronger, and they successfully crossed the chasm.

The spirit watched their progress with approval. "You have proven your worthiness. The knowledge and relics of this chamber are yours."

As they explored the hidden chamber, they discovered ancient tomes detailing powerful spells and techniques, relics imbued with magical energy, and records of their ancestors' achievements and struggles.

One particular tome caught Lydia's attention. It contained detailed accounts of a powerful artifact known as the Heart of Eternity—a crystal said to hold the essence of life and the key to unlocking untold power.

Elara carefully examined the glowing crystal on the pedestal. "This must be the Heart of Eternity. Its power could be a great asset, but it must be used wisely."

Marcus nodded; his expression serious. "We need to ensure it doesn't fall into the wrong hands. We'll study it and determine how best to use its power."

With their newfound knowledge and relics, the team returned to the mansion, their hearts filled with hope and determination. They knew that the Heart of Eternity and the secrets of the hidden chamber would be crucial in their ongoing efforts to protect their world.

Elara stood before her friends and allies, holding the Heart of Eternity. "We've uncovered incredible knowledge and power, but with it comes great responsibility. We must use it to honor our ancestors and protect the peace we've fought so hard to achieve."

The room erupted in applause, their commitment to their mission stronger than ever. They knew that the challenges ahead would be great, but they were ready to face them together.

As they settled into their new roles and responsibilities, Elara and her allies continued to strengthen their bonds and prepare for the future. They knew that the shadows of the past would always be a part of their journey, but with the knowledge and power they had gained, they were ready to face whatever came next.

Elara stood in the garden, looking out at the horizon. The sun was setting, casting a golden glow over the landscape. She felt a sense of peace and purpose, knowing that they were on the right path.

Marcus joined her, his presence a comforting anchor. "We've come a long way, Elara. And there's still so much more to do."

Elara smiled; her heart filled with hope. "Yes, there is. But with you and our friends by my side, I know we can achieve anything."

As the stars began to twinkle in the night sky, Elara and Marcus stood together, ready to face the future and the adventures it held. They knew that the echoes of the past would guide them, and the light of their vision would lead them forward.

Chapter 14
The Heart of Eternity

With the Heart of Eternity in their possession, Elara and her allies focused on understanding its power and potential. The crystal's essence seemed to pulse with a life of its own, radiating an energy that was both captivating and formidable. They knew that harnessing its power would require caution, wisdom, and unity.

The mansion became a hive of activity as the team delved into research and training. Lydia, with her vast knowledge of ancient texts and magical lore, took the lead in studying the Heart of Eternity. She spent long hours in the library, cross-referencing the new information with what they already knew.

Elara, Marcus, Theo, Jax, and Selena dedicated themselves to intensive training, honing their skills and learning how to work with the crystal's energy. They practiced new techniques, developed strategies, and prepared for any potential threats that might arise.

One evening, as Elara and Marcus were sparring in the training room, Lydia burst in, her face alight with excitement. "I've found something!" she exclaimed, holding an ancient tome.

Elara and Marcus paused; their curiosity piqued. "What is it?" Elara asked.

Lydia placed the tome on a nearby table and opened it to a specific page. "This text details the rituals and spells associated with the Heart of Eternity. It also mentions a location where we can find the final key to unlocking its full potential—a place called the Temple of Shadows."

Theo, who had been watching from the sidelines, raised an eyebrow. "The Temple of Shadows? Sounds ominous."

Lydia nodded. "It's an ancient site, hidden deep within a forest to the east. According to the text, the temple houses the final piece of the puzzle—a ritual that can awaken the true power of the Heart of Eternity."

Elara felt a surge of determination. "Then that's where we need to go. We'll prepare for the journey and set out as soon as possible."

The team set out at dawn, their destination the mysterious and ancient Temple of Shadows. The journey took them through dense forests, over rugged hills, and across rushing rivers. The landscape grew increasingly wild and untamed as they approached their goal.

As they traveled, they encountered various challenges—natural obstacles, treacherous terrain, and the occasional wild creature. Their skills and teamwork were tested, but their determination never wavered.

One evening, as they made camp by a clear, bubbling stream, Elara took a moment to reflect on their journey. She felt a deep connection to her friends and allies, knowing that together they could overcome any obstacle.

Marcus joined her by the stream, his presence a comforting anchor. "How are you feeling about this, Elara?" he asked, his voice gentle.

Elara smiled, looking out at the moonlit forest. "I'm ready. We've come so far, and I know we can do this. The Heart of Eternity is powerful, but with the right guidance, we can use it to protect our world."

Marcus nodded; his eyes filled with admiration. "You're an incredible leader, Elara. Whatever happens, we'll face it together."

After several days of travel, they finally reached the Temple of Shadows. The ancient structure was hidden deep within the forest, its dark stone walls covered in moss and vines. The air was thick with a sense of mystery and magic.

They approached the entrance cautiously, their senses alert for any signs of danger. The temple's interior was dimly lit by flickering torches, casting eerie shadows on the walls. As they ventured deeper, they encountered intricate carvings and symbols that hinted at the temple's long history and purpose.

In the heart of the temple, they found a grand chamber, its ceiling soaring high above them. At the center of the chamber stood an altar, surrounded by ancient runes and glowing with a faint, otherworldly light.

Lydia stepped forward; her voice filled with awe. "This is it. The ritual site described in the tome."

Elara placed the Heart of Eternity on the altar, feeling its energy resonate with the temple's magic. "What do we need to do?"

Lydia opened the tome and began to chant the ancient incantations. As she spoke, the runes around the altar began to glow brighter, and the air crackled with magical energy.

Suddenly, the ground shook, and a portal of swirling shadows appeared above the altar. From the portal emerged a figure, tall and imposing, its form shifting and changing like smoke.

"I am the Guardian of the Temple," the figure intoned, its voice echoing through the chamber. "To unlock the power of the Heart of Eternity, you must prove yourselves worthy."

The Guardian's challenge was a test of their unity, strength, and resolve. It conjured illusions and obstacles, forcing them to confront their deepest fears and greatest weaknesses.

Elara faced visions of her past, moments of doubt and failure. But she drew strength from her friends and allies, pushing through the illusions and emerging stronger.

Marcus and Theo battled their own fears, their trust in each other and their skills guiding them through the trials. Jax and Selena used their physical prowess and magical abilities to overcome the obstacles, their determination unwavering.

Lydia, focused and calm, continued to chant the incantations, guiding her friends with her wisdom and knowledge.

As they overcame the final challenge, the Guardian nodded in approval. "You have proven yourselves worthy. The power of the Heart of Eternity is yours to command."

The portal of shadows closed, and the Heart of Eternity began to glow with a brilliant light. Elara felt its energy surge through her, filling her with a sense of power and clarity.

With the Heart of Eternity fully awakened, the team returned to the mansion, their hearts filled with hope and determination. They knew that they now possessed a powerful tool to protect their world and uphold the peace they had fought so hard to achieve.

Elara stood before her friends and allies, holding the glowing crystal. "We've unlocked the power of the Heart of Eternity. With it, we can face any challenge and protect our world. But we must use it wisely, and always remember the lessons we've learned."

Marcus placed a hand on her shoulder, his voice filled with pride. "We will, Elara. Together, we can achieve anything."

As they celebrated their success, Elara felt a deep sense of fulfillment and purpose. The journey had been long and difficult, but they had emerged stronger, united by their shared vision and determination.

The future was bright, filled with possibilities and adventures. And with the Heart of Eternity by their side, Elara knew they were ready to face whatever came next.

Chapter 15
The Rising Storm

With the Heart of Eternity fully awakened, the team focused on utilizing its power to strengthen their defenses and ensure the peace they had worked so hard to achieve. However, a new threat was brewing on the horizon—a powerful and ancient force determined to reclaim the Heart of Eternity and plunge the world into chaos.

The days following their return from the Temple of Shadows were filled with preparations and training. The Heart of Eternity's power was integrated into their strategies, and the council worked tirelessly to ensure the stability of their alliance.

One afternoon, as Elara was reviewing plans with Marcus and Lydia, Gabriel, the vampire with an extensive network of spies, burst into the room, his expression grim.

"We have a problem," Gabriel said, his voice tense. "There's been an increase in unusual activity—sightings of strange creatures and reports of powerful magic being used. It seems like someone or something is gathering forces against us."

Elara's heart sank. "Do we know who or what is behind it?"

Gabriel shook his head. "Not yet, but it's clear that whoever it is, they're targeting the Heart of Eternity."

Lydia looked up from her notes, her eyes wide with concern. "Could it be related to the ancient enemy mentioned in the vault's texts? The one who sought the Heart of Eternity centuries ago?"

Elara nodded, her resolve hardening. "It's possible. We need to investigate and prepare for the worst. We can't let them succeed."

Elara and her team split up to gather more information. Marcus and Theo headed to the outskirts of the city, where the sightings had been reported. Lydia, Jax, and Selena stayed at the mansion to strengthen their magical defenses and prepare for any potential attacks.

As Marcus and Theo investigated, they encountered strange, otherworldly creatures—beings of shadow and darkness, unlike anything they had ever seen. The creatures seemed to be drawn to the Heart of Eternity's energy, their presence a clear sign of the rising threat.

One evening, as Elara and her allies were reviewing their findings, the mansion was suddenly attacked. Dark, shadowy figures swarmed the grounds, their eyes glowing with malevolent intent. The air crackled with dark magic, and the sky above the mansion darkened ominously.

Jax and Selena sprang into action, their combat skills and magical abilities driving back the attackers. Lydia used her spells to create protective barriers, while Marcus and Theo fought with relentless determination.

Elara, holding the Heart of Eternity, felt its power surge through her. She knew that this was the moment they had been preparing for—the true test of their strength and unity.

As the battle raged on, a figure emerged from the shadows—a tall, imposing being with eyes that glowed like embers. Elara recognized him from the ancient texts: Malakar, the ancient enemy who had once sought the Heart of Eternity.

Malakar's voice was cold and menacing. "The Heart of Eternity belongs to me. Hand it over, and I may spare your lives."

Elara stood her ground, her voice unwavering. "We will never let you have it.

The Heart of Eternity is meant to protect, not to destroy."

Malakar sneered. "Foolish child. You have no idea of its true power. But no matter—I will take it by force."

With a wave of his hand, Malakar unleashed a torrent of dark energy, aiming to overwhelm Elara and her allies. But Elara, channeling the Heart of Eternity's power, created a shield of light, deflecting the attack and protecting her friends.

The battle between light and darkness intensified, each side pushing their limits. Elara and her allies fought with everything they had, their unity and determination driving them forward.

As the fight continued, Elara realized that they needed to disrupt Malakar's connection to the dark magic. She called out to Lydia, who nodded and began chanting an incantation to weaken Malakar's power.

Selena joined in, adding her own magic to the spell. The combined forces of their magic began to take effect, and Malakar's dark energy wavered.

Seeing their opportunity, Marcus and Theo launched a coordinated attack, striking at Malakar's defenses. Jax, with his incredible strength, delivered a powerful blow that knocked Malakar off balance.

Elara, holding the Heart of Eternity, focused its energy into a concentrated beam of light. She aimed it at Malakar, pouring all her strength and resolve into the attack.

Malakar screamed in fury and pain as the light engulfed him, breaking his connection to the dark magic. With a final, defiant roar, he was consumed by the light and vanished, leaving behind only a lingering darkness that quickly dissipated.

The battle was over, and the mansion was once again secure. Elara and her allies stood together, their hearts filled with relief and triumph. They had faced a powerful enemy and emerged victorious, their unity and strength carrying them through.

Elara held the Heart of Eternity, feeling its energy settle into a calm, steady rhythm. She knew that the battle had been a turning point, a test of their resolve and their ability to protect their world.

Marcus placed a hand on her shoulder, his voice filled with pride. "We did it, Elara. We protected the Heart of Eternity and our home."

Lydia smiled, her eyes shining with happiness. "And we did it together. Our bond is our greatest strength."

Theo grinned; his usual charm evident. "To the future, and all the adventures it holds."

In the days that followed, the council worked to rebuild and strengthen their defenses, ensuring that they were prepared for any future threats. The alliance between the vampire clans grew stronger, their shared experiences forging an unbreakable bond.

Elara stood in the garden, looking out at the horizon. The sun was rising, casting a golden glow over the landscape. She felt a deep sense of peace and purpose, knowing that they were on the right path.

Marcus joined her, his presence a comforting anchor. "We've come a long way, Elara. And there's still so much more to do."

Elara smiled; her heart filled with hope. "Yes, there is. But with you and our friends by my side, I know we can achieve anything."

As the stars began to twinkle in the night sky, Elara and Marcus stood together, ready to face the future and the adventures it held. They knew that the Heart of Eternity would guide them, and the light of their vision would lead them forward.

Chapter 16
The Dawn of a New Era

The defeat of Malakar brought a sense of relief and renewed hope to Elara and her allies. With the Heart of Eternity secure and their bond stronger than ever, they began to look towards the future. They knew that their world would always face challenges, but they were ready to face them together.

The council gathered in the mansion's grand hall, their expressions a mix of determination and optimism. The battle with Malakar had shown them the importance of unity and the power of the Heart of Eternity. Now, they needed to ensure that their newfound strength was used to protect and build a brighter future.

Elara addressed the council, her voice clear and confident. "We've overcome great challenges and proven that our unity is our greatest strength. Now, we must look to the future. We need to continue strengthening our alliances and expanding our reach to ensure lasting peace."

Marcus nodded in agreement. "We should start by reaching out to other supernatural communities—those who have remained neutral or isolated. If we can bring them into our fold, we'll be even stronger."

Lydia added, "I've been studying the ancient texts, and there are mentions of powerful artifacts and knowledge scattered across the world. If we can find and secure them, it will further bolster our defenses."

Theo grinned. "Sounds like another adventure. I'm in."

The team split into smaller groups, each tasked with a different mission. Elara, Marcus, and Lydia set out to contact other supernatural communities, hoping to forge new alliances. Theo, Jax, and Selena embarked on a quest to locate and secure the mentioned artifacts.

Elara's group traveled to distant lands, meeting with leaders of various supernatural factions. They encountered werewolf packs, faerie courts, and ancient sorcerers, each with their own unique abilities and perspectives. Some were wary at first, but Elara's genuine passion and the proof of their success in defeating Malakar won many over.

One evening, as they sat around a campfire with a werewolf alpha named Rylan, Elara spoke of their vision for the future. "We're stronger together. Our differences are our strengths, and by uniting, we can protect our world from any threat."

Rylan nodded thoughtfully. "You've proven your strength and your commitment. We will stand with you."

Meanwhile, Theo, Jax, and Selena followed the clues from Lydia's research, traveling to ancient ruins and hidden caves. They faced numerous challenges—traps, guardians, and treacherous terrain—but their skills and teamwork saw them through.

In a forgotten temple deep within a jungle, they discovered a powerful amulet said to enhance magical abilities. In a desolate desert, they unearthed a staff that could control the elements. Each artifact they found added to their growing arsenal, making their alliance even more formidable.

With new alliances forged and powerful artifacts secured, Elara and her allies returned to the mansion. The council convened a great gathering, inviting representatives from all the supernatural factions they had reached out to. The atmosphere was charged with excitement and anticipation.

Elara stood before the assembled leaders, her heart swelling with pride and hope. "We have come together from all corners of the world, united by our shared vision of peace and protection. Together, we are unstoppable."

The leaders nodded in agreement, their faces reflecting their commitment to the new alliance. They discussed plans for joint training exercises, shared resources, and coordinated efforts to safeguard their world.

Later that evening, as the celebrations continued, Elara slipped away to the mansion's garden. The night was calm and the stars shone brightly above. She felt a deep sense of contentment and purpose, knowing that they had laid the foundation for a brighter future.

Marcus found her there, his presence a comforting anchor. "You did it, Elara. You brought us all together."

Elara smiled, leaning into him. "We did it, Marcus. And there's still so much more to do."

Marcus nodded, his eyes reflecting the light of the stars. "Yes, but I have no doubt we can handle it. Together."

In the days and weeks that followed, the new alliance began to take shape. Training sessions were held, knowledge was shared, and the bonds between the different factions grew stronger. The Heart of Eternity was used wisely, its power a beacon of hope and strength.

Elara and her allies continued to lead with courage and vision, always mindful of the lessons they had learned and the responsibilities they carried. They knew that the road ahead would be filled with challenges, but they were ready to face them together.

As Elara looked out at the horizon, she felt a sense of anticipation and excitement for the future. The dawn of a new era had begun, and with the Heart of Eternity and their united

front, they were prepared to protect and build
a world where all could thrive.

Chapter 17
The Eternal Guardians

With the new alliances firmly established and the Heart of Eternity as their guiding light, Elara and her allies found themselves at the forefront of a rapidly evolving world. As they worked to strengthen their defenses and maintain the delicate balance between the various supernatural factions, a new challenge emerged—one that would test their unity and resolve in ways they had never imagined.

One afternoon, as Elara and Lydia were discussing the latest developments in their research, a young scout burst into the room, out of breath and visibly shaken.

"Lady Elara, we have a visitor," the scout panted. "He claims to be an emissary from an ancient order and insists on speaking with you immediately."

Elara exchanged a concerned glance with Lydia before nodding. "Bring him in."

The scout led the way, and moments later, a tall, cloaked figure entered the room. His eyes, sharp and intelligent, surveyed the surroundings before settling on Elara.

"I am Aric, an emissary of the Eternal Guardians," the man said, his voice calm and steady. "We have watched your efforts and believe it is time for our paths to cross."

Elara's curiosity was piqued. "The Eternal Guardians? I've heard of them only in legends. What brings you here?"

Aric reached into his cloak and produced a small, intricately carved box. "The Heart of Eternity is a powerful artifact, but it is only one piece of a greater puzzle. We possess knowledge and relics that can enhance its power and protect it from those who seek to misuse it."

Elara, Marcus, Lydia, and Theo traveled with Aric to the Eternal Guardians' sanctuary, a hidden stronghold nestled deep within an ancient forest. The sanctuary was a marvel of both nature and magic, with towering trees and shimmering barriers protecting it from the outside world.

The leader of the Eternal Guardians, a wise and venerable woman named Seraphina, greeted them with warmth and respect. "Welcome, Elara. We have long awaited the day when our paths would converge."

Seraphina led them to a grand hall, where artifacts and tomes from countless eras were displayed. "The Heart of Eternity is powerful, but it is vulnerable to corruption. With our guidance, you can unlock its full potential and safeguard it from those who would use it for evil."

Over the next several weeks, Elara and her allies immersed themselves in the teachings of the Eternal Guardians. They learned new techniques for channeling and protecting the Heart of Eternity's energy, and they trained alongside the Guardians, honing their skills and deepening their understanding of their shared mission.

One evening, as Elara practiced a particularly complex ritual with Seraphina, she felt a profound connection to the Heart of Eternity. The crystal's energy flowed through her, filling her with a sense of clarity and purpose.

"You are its chosen guardian, Elara," Seraphina said softly. "With your leadership, the Heart of Eternity will become a beacon of hope and strength for all."

As their training with the Eternal Guardians progressed, news of a new threat reached the sanctuary. A powerful sorcerer named Kael, who had long been rumored to be gathering dark forces, had surfaced and was seeking to claim the Heart of Eternity for himself.

Aric brought the news to Elara and her team. "Kael is a formidable enemy, with knowledge of ancient, forbidden magic. He has already amassed a significant following and poses a great danger to our world."

Elara felt a chill run down her spine. "We must stop him. The Heart of Eternity cannot fall into his hands."

Marcus nodded; his expression resolute. "We'll need to gather our allies and prepare for battle. This will be our greatest challenge yet."

Returning to the mansion, Elara and her allies called upon the supernatural factions they had united. Leaders from the werewolf packs, faerie courts, and other supernatural communities arrived, ready to stand against the looming threat.

In the grand hall, Elara addressed the assembled leaders. "Kael seeks to destroy everything we have built. But together, we are strong. We will stand united and protect our world from his darkness."

The leaders pledged their support, and preparations for the battle began in earnest. Training sessions were intensified, defenses were fortified, and strategies were developed. The Heart of Eternity's power was harnessed to its fullest, enhancing their abilities and strengthening their resolve.

The day of the battle arrived, and Elara's forces faced Kael's dark army on a desolate battlefield. The air crackled with tension and magic; the sky darkened by storm clouds that mirrored the conflict below.

Elara stood at the forefront, the Heart of Eternity glowing with a brilliant light. Beside her were Marcus, Lydia, Theo, Jax, Selena, and the leaders of their allied factions. They were ready to face whatever came next, their unity and determination unwavering.

Kael, a tall and imposing figure with eyes that burned like fire, stepped forward, his voice echoing with malice. "You cannot stop me, Elara. The Heart of Eternity will be mine, and I will remake this world in my image."

Elara's voice rang out strong and clear. "We stand together, Kael. You will not prevail."

The battle erupted with a fury unlike any they had faced before. Magic clashed with magic, and the air was filled with the sounds of combat and the cries of the wounded. Elara, channeling the Heart of Eternity, led her forces with courage and strength.

As the battle raged on, Elara and Kael faced each other, their powers colliding in a dazzling display of light and dark. Kael's dark magic was formidable, but Elara's connection to the Heart of Eternity gave her an edge.

With a final, desperate effort, Elara focused all her energy into a beam of pure light, aimed directly at Kael. The light engulfed him, shattering his dark magic and breaking his hold over his forces.

Kael screamed in fury and agony as the light consumed him, his form disintegrating into nothingness. The dark army, leaderless and defeated, scattered and fled.

The battlefield fell silent as the last of Kael's forces disappeared. Elara's allies cheered in victory, their unity and strength having carried them through the darkest of times.

Elara stood among her friends and allies, the Heart of Eternity glowing softly in her hand. Marcus approached her, his eyes filled with pride and relief. "We did it, Elara. We protected our world."

Lydia, Theo, Jax, and Selena joined them, their faces reflecting the same sense of triumph and hope. "This is just the beginning," Lydia said with a smile. "Together, we can face anything."

In the days that followed, the council and their allies worked to rebuild and strengthen their world. The victory over Kael had solidified their unity and demonstrated the power of their alliance.

Elara stood in the garden of the mansion, looking out at the horizon as the sun rose, casting a golden glow over the landscape. She felt a deep sense of peace and purpose, knowing that they had laid the foundation for a brighter future.

Marcus joined her, his presence a comforting anchor. "We've come a long way, Elara. And there's still so much more to do."

Elara smiled; her heart filled with hope. "Yes, there is. But with you and our friends by my side, I know we can achieve anything."

As the stars began to twinkle in the night sky, Elara and Marcus stood together, ready to face the future and the adventures it held. They knew that the Heart of Eternity would guide them, and the light of their vision would lead them forward.

Chapter 18
Solidifying the Alliance

The victory over Kael was a turning point for Elara and her allies. With the threat defeated, they turned their attention to solidifying the alliance and ensuring the lasting peace they had fought so hard to achieve.

The grand hall of the mansion was filled with representatives from all the allied factions. The air was charged with a sense of purpose and optimism as they gathered to discuss their future.

Elara stood at the head of the table, her presence commanding and reassuring. "We've achieved a great victory, but our work is far from over. To ensure lasting peace, we must continue to strengthen our bonds and work together."

Marcus nodded, his voice steady. "We propose the formation of a council, with representatives from each faction. This council will oversee our collective efforts and ensure that we remain united."

Lydia added, "The Heart of Eternity will remain a symbol of our unity and a tool to protect us. We will use its power wisely and for the benefit of all."

The leaders of the various factions voiced their agreement, and the council was officially formed. Each faction chose a representative to serve on the council, ensuring that every voice would be heard.

In the weeks that followed, the council worked tirelessly to implement new structures and strategies. They established communication networks, coordinated training programs, and developed plans for joint defense.

Theo took on the role of liaison, using his charm and diplomacy to facilitate cooperation between the factions. Jax and

Selena led training exercises, sharing their skills and knowledge with the allied forces.

Elara and Marcus focused on strengthening the magical defenses around their territories, with Lydia's guidance. The Heart of Eternity played a crucial role, its power enhancing their efforts and ensuring the security of their world.

One evening, as the sun set over the mansion, Elara took a moment to reflect on her journey. She stood in the garden, the Heart of Eternity glowing softly in her hand.

Marcus joined her, his presence a comforting anchor. "You've come a long way, Elara. From discovering your heritage to leading this incredible alliance. I'm proud of you."

Elara smiled, feeling a deep sense of gratitude. "I couldn't have done it without you and our friends. We've built something truly remarkable together."

To celebrate their achievements and the formation of the council, the allied factions held a grand festival. The mansion and its grounds were transformed with lights, music, and laughter. Representatives from all factions mingled, their differences set aside in a show of unity.

Elara stood on a raised platform, addressing the gathered crowd. "Tonight, we celebrate not just our victory, but our unity. We are stronger together, and we will continue to protect and build a future where all can thrive."

The crowd erupted in cheers, their voices a testament to their shared commitment and hope.

As the festival continued, Elara and Marcus found a quiet spot to talk. "We've accomplished so much, but there's still more to do," Marcus said, his eyes reflecting the light of the stars.

Elara nodded; her heart filled with determination. "Yes, but I know we can handle it. Together, we'll face whatever comes next."

In the distance, Lydia, Theo, Jax, and Selena were laughing and talking, their bond unbreakable. Elara felt a deep sense of peace and purpose, knowing that they were ready for whatever the future held.

Chapter 19
A Peaceful Future

With the council established and the alliances strong, Elara and her allies focused on maintaining the peace and continuing their efforts to protect their world. The bonds they had forged and the lessons they had learned would guide them as they moved forward.

The daily life of the mansion and its inhabitants became a testament to their unity and resilience. Training sessions, council meetings, and joint missions became routine, each day strengthening their resolve and their bond.

Elara took on the role of mentor and leader, guiding new recruits and sharing her experiences. Marcus worked closely with the council, ensuring that their strategies were effective and that their goals were aligned.

Lydia delved deeper into her studies of ancient texts and magic, always seeking ways to improve their defenses and expand their knowledge. Theo continued to build bridges between the factions, his charm and diplomacy invaluable.

Jax and Selena focused on training and preparedness, their skills ensuring that their forces were always ready for any threat.

One evening, as the sun set over the horizon, Elara gathered with her closest friends in the garden. They sat around a fire, sharing stories and reflecting on their journey.

"We've come so far," Lydia said, her voice filled with pride. "We've faced incredible challenges and emerged stronger."

Theo nodded. "And we've done it together. That's what makes us unstoppable."

Jax raised a glass. "To our future and the adventures, it holds."

Elara looked around at her friends, her heart filled with gratitude and hope. "We've built something truly remarkable. And I know that whatever comes next, we'll face it together."

As the night turned to dawn, Elara stood at the edge of the garden, watching the sunrise. The first light of day cast a golden glow over the landscape, a symbol of the new era they had ushered in.

Marcus joined her, his presence a comforting anchor. "The future is bright, Elara. We've achieved so much, and there's still so much more to do."

Elara smiled; her heart filled with determination. "Yes, but with you and our friends by my side, I know we can achieve anything."

As the stars faded and the sun rose higher, Elara and Marcus stood together, ready to face the future and the adventures it held. They knew that the Heart of Eternity would guide them, and the light of their vision would lead them forward.

Years later, the alliance between the supernatural factions had grown even stronger. The council, led by Elara and her allies, had successfully maintained peace and prosperity. The Heart of Eternity remained a symbol of unity and strength, its power a beacon of hope for all.

Elara walked through the halls of the mansion, now a thriving center of cooperation and learning. She paused by a window, looking out at the bustling grounds filled with supernatural beings working together.

Marcus approached, his smile warm and reassuring. "We've come a long way, Elara. And it's all because of your vision and leadership."

Elara turned to him, her heart filled with gratitude and love. "It's because of all of us.

We've built something truly remarkable together."

As they stood together, watching the future unfold before them, Elara knew that their legacy would endure. They had faced incredible challenges and emerged stronger, united by their shared vision and determination.

The future was bright, filled with endless possibilities and adventures. And with the Heart of Eternity and their unbreakable bond, Elara and her allies were ready to face whatever came next.